D1580322

Raja's Pet CAMEL

The Magic of Hope

BY Anita Nahta Amin

Illustrated BY Parwinder Singh

RAJA'S PET CAMEL
The Magic of Hope

Copyright 2020 by Anita Nahta Amin
All rights reserved. First Edition.
Printed in China and published by Cardinal Rule Press

Summary: A little boy in India must find a way to keep his mischievous pet camel when his father decides to sell it.

Our books may be purchased in bulk for promotional, educational or business use. Please contact your local bookseller or IPG Books at orders@ipgbook.com.

Library of Congress Control Number: 2019950695
ebook: ISBN: 978-1-7330359-3-4
hardcover: ISBN: 978-1-7330359-4-1
softcover: ISBN: 978-1-7330359-5-8

The art in this book was created using digital pencil in Procreate and Photoshop.

Book design by: Maggie Villaume

CARDINAL RULE PRESS

5449 Sylvia
Dearborn Heights, MI 48125
Visit us at www.CardinalRulePress.com

Before Reading:

- This story takes place in India. Help your child find India on a map.
- Read the title with your child. How would they name a book about their pet? Discuss your pet's personality. If you don't have a pet, talk about what type of pet your child might want and why.

During Reading:

- Ask your child: How does Raja's life in India differ from your own?
- Kamal the camel is far from perfect. Discuss how pets and people are never perfect.
- Taking care of Kamal is a lot of hard work! Ask your child to list what they do to take care of their pet - or what they would do if they had one.

After Reading:

- Kamal the camel is naughty. Ask your child: Do you think Kamal will ever change? Why or why not? Discuss what they've learned this year and how learning has helped them change and grow.
- Discuss how Raja didn't give up and why perseverance is important. Talk about something your child has accomplished by not giving up.
- Taste some dates and see if your family enjoys them as much as Raja's family - especially Kamal! Bonus points if your child tries lentils or other Indian food, too!

For my darling husband Jay, our beautiful kids Asha & Ajay, and my brave parents, Roop & Binata

····· Anita Amin

To Kamal (the camel in this book) - I would love to see you during my next visit to Rajasthan!

····· Parwinder Singh

As Raja walked home from school, a lone baby camel cried. *Me-yoo... Me-yoo...*

"Are you scared?" Raja asked. He tried to pet it. But it kicked sand at him and skittered away... until it noticed his shiny lunch tin.

"Are you hungry?" Raja fed the camel leftover lentils
and dates. It gulped down all of the dates.

They played fetch, chase, and hide-and-seek,
and cuddled under a tree.

When Raja got up to leave, the camel followed him home.

"I will name you Kamal. You can be my pet." Raja had always wanted to have a pet - like the happy kids in his school books did. But most yard animals in India worked. They didn't just play.

At home, his father, Bapu, frowned. "We don't have time for camels. We're too busy herding goats."

But when Raja kept pleading, "Pleeeease?" and Kamal refused to "go home," and no one came to claim her, Bapu said, "It can stay until we find a home for it."

But Kamal was a wild camel with wild ways.

She ate Bapu's dates, chased their goats, knocked down fences, drank all their water, smashed clay pots, and spit at neighbors.

After a week of missing snacks, losing goats, mending fences, hauling well water, patching pots, and apologizing to neighbors, Bapu cried, "This camel is too much trouble! We're selling it at the fair."

The fair was only weeks away. Raja was heartbroken... until he remembered the camel race there. "We could win big money!" Raja told Kamal. "Then Bapu will be so pleased, he'll never want to sell you!"

They trained every afternoon during Bapu's naptime.

Raja pulled and pushed Kamal.

Kamal wouldn't move.

Raja scolded and coaxed Kamal.

Kamal still wouldn't move.

Raja took a break and ate dates. Kamal wanted some!

"I think we can win!" Kamal was a fast runner
when dates were the prize...

Five days before the fair, Bapu, Raja, Kamal,
and a handful of goats set out across the desert.
They walked for several days and nights.

Along the way, people stopped to admire Kamal.

And Raja worried. "I don't want anyone to buy her."
"They can give it a good home," Bapu said.
So can we, Raja thought, dragging his feet.

Finally, they arrived at the fair. They weaved between
tents and passed campfires spitting black smoke.
Raja felt even smaller in the crowd of tabla drummers,
sitar strummers, snake charmers, magicians,
acrobats, and more.

Bapu found a good spot and set up their tent.
He dressed Kamal in her finest jewelry.

Raja couldn't let anyone buy Kamal!

"She spits," Raja whispered to one buyer.

"She snores," he told another. "Your village will never sleep."

"She's rude," he told a mustachioed man. "Goats are nicer."

Bapu sold all of his goats.
He was happy.

No one bought Kamal. Raja was happy...

Until Bapu said, "Tomorrow is the busiest day of the fair. Someone will surely buy this camel then."

Raja didn't sleep that night. Tomorrow was race day. After that, he might never see Kamal again.

As soon as the sun rose, Raja hurried to the fruit stand for dates.

"I just sold the last bag," the fruit seller said.

No dates for Kamal?

They had no choice. They lined up at the race track.
The other camels towered over Kamal.

"But you're faster," Raja told her.

The starter waved his flag. And then, a stampede!
Camel after camel roared past Raja and Kamal.

"Go, Kamal. We have to win!" Raja shouted.

The sun burned Raja's head. Sweat poured down his neck. He choked on the dust. But the soft pounding of camel feet grew louder and louder. Kamal was catching up.

Then Raja saw the mustachioed man - in the crowd - eating dates! "No!" Raja cried. But it was too late.

The crowd screamed and scattered.
Kamal chased the man and wolfed down his dates.

"That is a bad camel!" The mustachioed man stomped away.

Raja wiped away his tears. "We lost, Kamal."
Kamal gave a sad bellow and a burp.

"No one will buy this camel now," Bapu grumbled.
"It scared everyone. It has no manners."

Raja felt a flash of hope. "I can teach her manners. She's just a baby. She'll learn. Just like she learned to race. Maybe she'll even learn to guard the goats."

Bapu liked this idea. "We'll give her one more try."

Raja leaped with joy! He kissed Bapu's feet
and hugged Kamal.

Then they packed up their tent. And Kamal,
now full of dates, obeyed Raja and Bapu...

...most of the way home.

10 Facts

- Many generations of a family - grandparents, parents, uncles, aunts, brothers, sisters, and cousins - live together in the same house.

- Most Indians don't own pets to just play with. Camels give milk to drink, pull carts, transport people, and give fur to weave into rope, among other jobs.

- Traditionally, Indians eat with their right hand - not with a fork or spoon. This includes eating soup, which can be mixed with rice to make it easier to scoop up!

- Indians celebrate when it finally rains. People dance and play in the rain - a fun way to cool down!

- When it is too hot inside, Indians sleep on cots or mats on the rooftop.

10 Facts

About the Thar Desert in India

- Many generations of a family - grandparents, parents, uncles, aunts, brothers, sisters, and cousins - live together in the same house.

- Most Indians don't own pets to just play with. Camels give milk to drink, pull carts, transport people, and give fur to weave into rope, among other jobs.

- Traditionally, Indians eat with their right hand - not with a fork or spoon. This includes eating soup, which can be mixed with rice to make it easier to scoop up!

- Indians celebrate when it finally rains. People dance and play in the rain - a fun way to cool down!

- When it is too hot inside, Indians sleep on cots or mats on the rooftop.

- Many homes don't have running water or stable electricity - no air conditioning or refrigerators. On special occasions, slabs of ice can be carted from a factory and cracked at home for a cold drink.

- To take an Indian-style bath, pour a few cups of cool water from a bucket over yourself.

- Most people don't own cars. You might walk or ride a scooter, bicycle, three-wheeled taxi, camel, bullock cart, or an open-air carriage pulled by a runner - while sharing the road with cows, donkeys, goats, monkeys, and peacocks.

- The tabla (tuh-bluh) is an Indian drum, thumped by the drummer's hands. The sitar (sih-tar) is about four feet tall, with strings that are plucked to make music.

- Indians leave their doors open during the day to cool their homes and welcome visitors. But cows are plentiful and roam free and sometimes wander in!

Anita Nahta Amin

Anita Nahta Amin is the author of several forthcoming chapter books and many short stories for children. Her work has been featured in a variety of children's literary magazines. This is her first picture book. Her family roots stretch across India from the vibrant camel-filled desert in Rajasthan to the bustling river city of Kolkata. She lives in Florida with her husband and twin children. She would love a pet camel too, as long as it doesn't eat all of her dates.

Parwinder Singh

Born and brought up in the Steel City, Jamshedpur, drawing and coloring has been Parwinder's hobby and passion since childhood. Spending the early years of his career in classical 2D animation and fascinated by various styles of illustrations, he was ultimately driven to the beautiful world of children's books. Freelancing has given him the chance he always wanted - he is able to explore more subjects and travel to different places.